SLEEPY KITTENS

JILL AND MARTIN LEMAN

TAMBOURINE BOOKS · NEW YORK

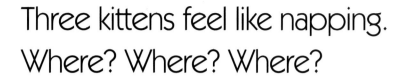

Three kittens feel like napping.
Where? Where? Where?

Up on the table,

Or down on the chair.

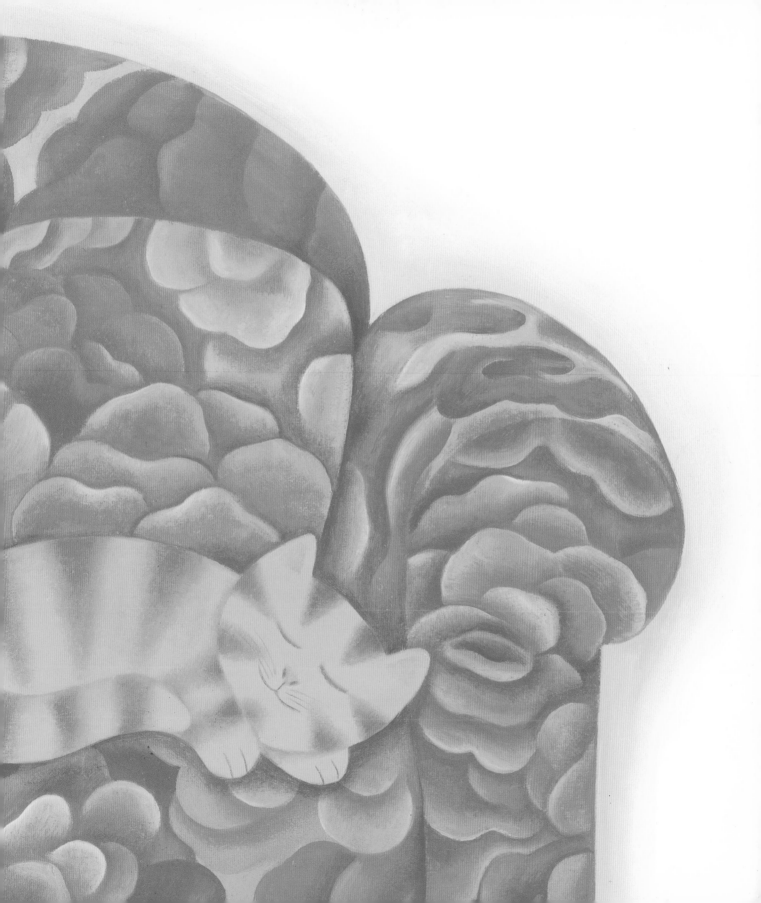

Under Mommy's sewing,

All over Granny's hat,

Snuggling next to Fido,

Or across a cuddly lap.

In front of a warm hearth,

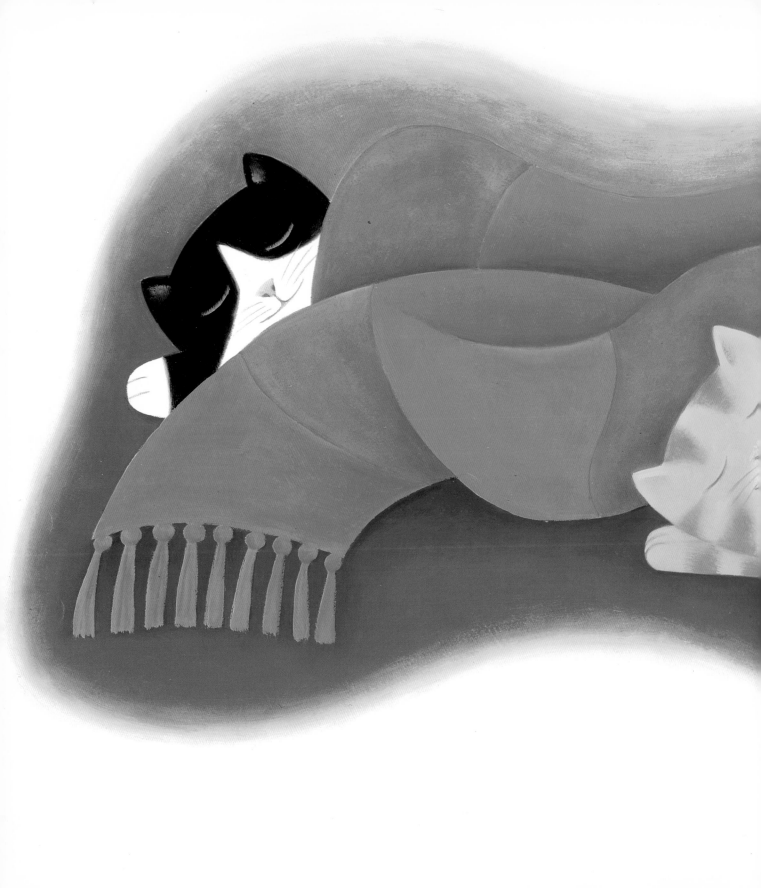

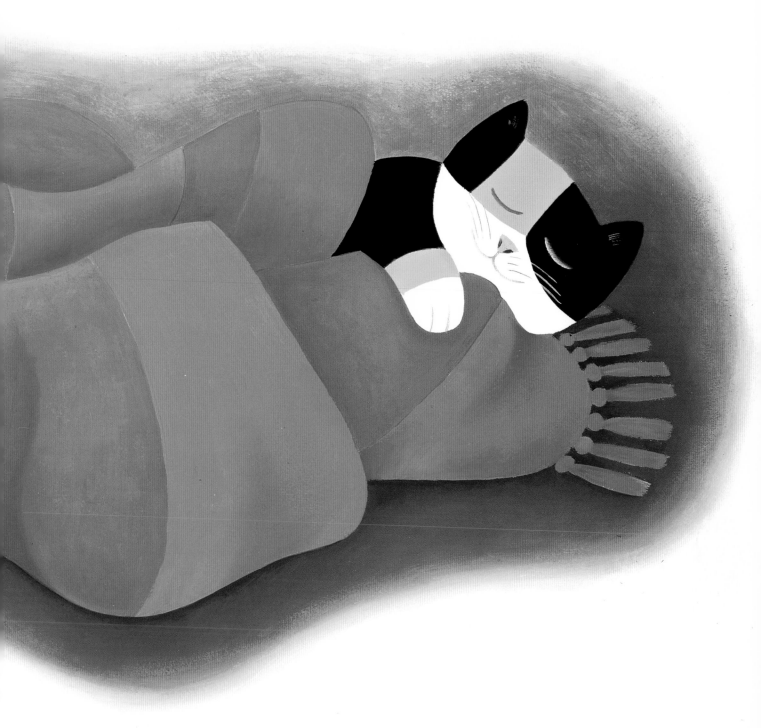

Or behind a woolly scarf,

Or in a drawer
between the socks,

But never in their special box!

They're always where they shouldn't be,

Even in my bed with me. Good night!